Barbie as
The Island Princess

Barbie as The Island Princess

Adapted by Judy Katschke
Based on the original screenplay
by Cliff Ruby & Elana Lesser

SCHOLASTIC INC.

New York   Toronto   London   Auckland   Sydney
Mexico City   New Delhi   Hong Kong   Buenos Aires

ISBN-13: 978-0-439-02548-5
ISBN-10: 0-439-02548-6

Special thanks to Vicki Jaeger, Monica Okazaki, Rob Hudnut, Shelley Dvi-Vardhana, Jesyca C. Durchin, Jennifer Twiner McCarron, Shea Wageman, Sharan Wood, Trevor Wyatt, Greg Richardson, Sean Newton, Kelsey Ayukawa, Luke DeWinter, Richard Dixon, Michael Douglas, Scott Eade, Derek Goodfellow, Shaun Martens, Chris McNish, Sarah Miyashita, Pam Prostarr, Craig Shiells, Sheila Turner, Lan Yao, and Walter P. Martishius.

Published by Scholastic Inc.
SCHOLASTIC and associated logos are trademarks and/or
registered trademarks of Scholastic Inc.

12 11 10 9 8 7 6 5 4 3 2 1   7 8 9 10 11/0

Printed in the U.S.A.
First printing, August 2007

Barbie as™
The Island Princess

Introduction

Once upon a time a tropical island shimmered on the ocean like a precious jewel. The island was home to many exotic plants, flowers, and animals. Two of those animals were Sagi the wise red panda and Azul the princely peacock.

One morning after a terrible storm, Sagi and Azul found the ruins of a shipwreck half-buried in the sands. There was a shiny hand mirror and a trunk filled with necklaces and lacy dresses. The trunk was marked with the letters "R" and "O."

Draped across the trunk was a flag displaying the emblem of a white rose. But their most curious find was an unconscious child who appeared to have been swept in from the sea.

Sagi and Azul carried the sleeping child to the small banyan tree where they lived. There they nursed her back to health. Over the years the tree grew sturdy and strong. So did the girl. The animals named her Ro for the letters on the trunk she had appeared with. Ro loved her island and her friends. But deep in her heart she wished to know where she truly came from. What Ro did find on her island was adventure!

Chapter 1

Ro gave a hearty wave to the chattering dolphins as she raced along the beach. The tropical sun cast its rays on the sparkling blue ocean. A warm breeze whistled through the towering palms while the wild island rose filled the air with its sweet perfume.

To most, such an island would be paradise. But to sixteen-year-old Ro, her island was also one big playground!

With her sun-streaked hair streaming behind her, Ro loved swinging on the vines

with her friends. She loved splashing in the watering hole with Tika the baby elephant, and sunning on the beach with Azul. She even loved hurling branches like high-flying javelins through the air.

That afternoon while Ro and her friends frolicked on the beach, they spotted something strange floating toward their island. Quickly, they made their way to the top of a bluff where they watched a huge hulking object drift into the cove.

"I've never seen a floating island before!" Azul exclaimed.

"That's not an island," Ro said. She wrinkled her nose as she thought hard. "It's a . . . hmmm."

Ro couldn't find the word. She knew she had seen one before — but where? Or when?

Suddenly, two strangers stepped off the ship, for that's what the object was, and onto the island. Sagi, Azul, and Tika stared down in amazement as one of the strangers made his way through the jungle. They had never seen such an animal before. It had no feathers, trunk, or tail. It wasn't a fish, and it certainly wasn't a whale.

"It can't be good," a worried Sagi said.

But Ro was not afraid as she climbed down the bluff for a closer look. To her, there was something wonderful about this strange new animal.

"He looks like me!" Ro said excitedly.

Way below, the stranger, who was named Antonio, had no idea he was being watched. He trekked through a tangle of thick jungle vines. After weeks at sea, it felt good to be on dry land.

The second stranger rushed to catch up to Antonio. This stranger was Antonio's friend Frazer. Frazer was a scientist and never went anywhere without his magnifying glass.

"Huge specimens of Palmaceae!" Frazer declared. He was about to inspect an odd-looking plant when both friends went crashing through a tangle of vines.

"Whoaaa!" Antonio and Frazer shouted.

They slipped down a steep muddy hill and tumbled over the edge of a cliff. Their wild ride came to an end as they splashed down into a thick, murky swamp!

Antonio and Frazer sat up, dripping with mud. But just when they thought they were alone, they were greeted by a group of hungry crocodiles.

One crocodile jumped up, snapping its jaws. Thinking fast, Antonio broke off a branch and jabbed it like a sword. But the weapon was no match for the crocodile and its razor-sharp teeth.

Antonio and Frazer knew they were in trouble, but suddenly Ro jumped out of nowhere onto a nearby rock. Shaking her finger at the crocodiles, she shouted: "Riki, Taj, Kiki, that's enough!"

Antonio watched in amazement as the creatures shut their huge gaping mouths. Was this girl actually talking to the crocodiles?

"Who are you?" Antonio asked.

"Who are *you*?" Ro asked back.

Ro led Antonio and Frazer back to the banyan tree and showed them her trunk. Antonio brushed his fingers over the letters.

"Ro," he read aloud. "Is that your name?"

"I think so," Ro replied. "Sagi tells me I came from the sea a long time ago," Ro explained.

"You don't remember? Perhaps a shipwreck," Antonio guessed. He became fascinated with Ro. And when he met Sagi, Azul, and Tika, he got an idea. . . .

"You saved us, now let us save you," Antonio said. "Come back to my kingdom."

"I still don't know your name," Ro said.

With a sweep of his arm, Frazer announced, "May I introduce Prince Antonio of the kingdom of Appolonia!"

Azul's eyes lit up. If Antonio was a prince, perhaps they were related!

"Ro, come with us to civilization," Antonio said.

Ro stared at the handsome prince with

the sparkling eyes and kind smile. She didn't want to leave her beloved island. But what if her real family was somewhere beyond the sea?

After much thought, Ro accepted the prince's invitation. Then she and her family of friends prepared to set sail!

Chapter 2

The next day the royal ship sailed away from the island. While Antonio gazed at the rolling sea through his spyglass, Ro gazed at Antonio.

"Why does he look through circles?" Ro wondered. She looked down at his boots. "And why does he cover his feet?"

Ro didn't understand many things about Antonio. But most of all, she didn't understand the butterflies she felt when she was near him.

Meanwhile, Antonio was starting to

have the same feelings for Ro. He had never met anyone so bold and daring. Or so lovely!

"Do you think she might like me?" Antonio asked Frazer.

The scientist rolled his eyes. Lovestruck princes were such peculiar specimens!

The ship sailed for many days. Then one day the royal ship sailed into Appolonia. Sagi, Azul, and Tika stood on the deck and watched as villagers hurried to welcome their prince and his ship.

"Everybody's like me!" Ro exclaimed, looking at all the people.

"But nobody's like me," Tika sighed. "Let's go home."

Ro couldn't figure out why Tika was so homesick. Where was the baby elephant's sense of adventure?

Suddenly, a little barn swallow crashed into one of the ship's sails. She bounced off it and landed on the deck right at Ro's feet.

"Are you all right?" Ro asked.

"Good as new!" she said as she ruffled her feathers. "I'm Tiny."

"Hello, Tiny. It's very nice to meet you. I'm Ro." The swallow smiled and then fluttered off.

The gangplank dropped and the

passengers stepped off the ship. The villagers couldn't stop staring at Ro and her odd pets. Who was this strange island girl?

Antonio's younger sisters ran up to greet them. Their names were Gina, Rita, and Sofia. They thought Ro and her animals were amazing, especially when Ro offered them a ride on Tika's back!

"I can't wait for you to meet my parents," Antonio told Ro.

While Azul rode in the royal carriage, Ro chose to ride Tika to the castle gates.

Upon entering the castle, Ro's eyes opened wide. She couldn't remember ever seeing anything so grand in her life.

Antonio introduced Ro to his parents

and Ro politely greeted King Peter and Queen Danielle. But when she met Tallulah, the queen's pet monkey, she knew she had made a new friend!

"I come from across the sea," Tallulah explained. To everyone in the room Tallulah's voice sounded like monkey chatter. Everyone, that is, except Ro, who understood her perfectly.

Ro smiled. The little white monkey was wearing satin bows and a tiny tiara.

"We're from across the sea, too!" Ro said excitedly.

The king and queen watched openmouthed as Ro spoke to Tallulah.

"Ro actually talks to animals," Antonio explained.

King Peter and Queen Danielle were surprised to meet such an unusual girl. But they had a surprise of their own.

"Antonio, I have important news," King Peter said. "A cause for celebration!"

The king rang a bell and the butler flung open the doors. In walked a stunning young woman. She was dressed in a long elegant gown and her dark shiny hair was styled to perfection.

"Son," King Peter said with a grin, "I am

delighted to introduce Princess Luciana, your bride-to-be."

"My what?" Antonio cried.

Ro was shocked, too. Why hadn't Antonio told her he was about to get married?

"And here is Luciana's mother, Queen Ariana," King Peter added.

Everyone turned. Framed in the doorway was a tall woman wearing a haughty expression and a very snug dress.

"An honor to meet my future son-in-law," Queen Ariana said. She whirled around as she admired the throne room. "I can see it now — everyone gathered here for the Royal Engagement Ball tomorrow!"

"Tomorrow?" Antonio exclaimed.

Ro felt her heart break into a million pieces. She wanted to return to her island

more than anything, but the next boat wasn't leaving for another two weeks.

What was I thinking? Ro wondered.

Prince Antonio belonged in this kingdom. She did not!

Chapter 3

Ro decided to make the best of this strange new world. She refused a room in the castle, choosing instead to stay with Sagi, Azul, and Tika in the royal greenhouse.

"Now this is a place for a royal bird!" Azul exclaimed.

Ro gazed around the sun-drenched glass building. It was filled with exotic flowers and plants — like the delicate island rose — that made her feel right at home.

"I can't wait until we go home," Tika sighed.

Ro wanted to go home, too, but she also wanted to find her real family. If only she knew where to start looking.

The door of the greenhouse suddenly opened. Tika frowned when she saw Prince Antonio standing there. What did he want now?

"I want my parents to know you the way I do," Antonio told Ro. He then invited her for tea in the gazebo.

Ro did not know what tea was, but she decided to find out. Later that day she found herself at an elegant table with Prince Antonio, King Peter, Queen Danielle, Queen Ariana, and her daughter Princess Luciana.

The royal butler walked around the table carefully pouring tea into each cup. Ro leaned over and noisily sniffed her tea.

Then she lapped at it with her tongue like a puppy dog!

"Ouch!" Ro said. The tea was hot. But the stares she got from King Peter, Queen Danielle, and Queen Ariana were icy cold!

"Ro grew up on an island in the South Seas," Antonio explained.

"You can hardly tell," Queen Ariana muttered.

Ro felt her cheeks burn. Perhaps this tea party was a bad idea!

"Watch me," Luciana whispered across the table. She lifted her teacup by its delicate handle. Then, with her pinky held up, she took a tiny sip.

"Thank you," Ro whispered back. She lifted her own teacup and did exactly the same. After taking a sip, Ro and Luciana smiled at each other across the table.

Queen Ariana was not smiling. The last thing she had expected was a rival for her daughter. She reached quietly under the table for her parasol. When the royal butler entered the room with a large tray of food, she stuck it out, tripping him. Cakes and fruits tumbled off his tray — and all over Ro's head and lap!

"Oh!" Ro gasped as sticky white icing dripped down her face.

Queen Ariana tried hard not to laugh.

She had never been so pleased. But Ro had never been so embarrassed in her life!

"I — I should be going," Ro stammered.

Before Antonio could stop her, Ro ran out of the gazebo, all the way to the greenhouse. Inside, the drooping plants looked exactly the way she felt: terrible!

As Ro watered the wilting island rose, she began singing the words to her favorite lullaby. She didn't know where she had learned the lullaby, but she remembered every note. . . .

"'It's magic when you are here beside me. Close your eyes and let me hold you tight,'" Ro sang. She watched the flowers and plants begin to bloom. But deep inside, her heart was withering. Why couldn't she do anything right in this kingdom?

Ro was about to tend to a fig tree when she spotted Tallulah in the greenhouse.

"My brother and I used to climb trees to pick figs," the little monkey said.

Ro pointed way up to the top of the tree. "The ripe fig is on the highest branch," she said. "It's all yours if you want it."

"You mean climb up there?" Tallulah gasped. "I'm afraid I've forgotten how."

Ro felt sorry for Tallulah. Monkeys ought to be climbing trees, not polishing their tiaras!

"We can fix that," Ro said with a smile.

She quickly schooled Tallulah in the art of tree climbing. It wasn't long before Ro and the little white monkey were swinging from tree to tree on the castle grounds!

"Is that what I think it is?" Queen Ariana said with a sneer as she watched.

Antonio smiled when he saw Ro swinging gracefully through the trees. What a fascinating and adventurous girl!

But King Peter had had enough of this monkey business. There would be no wild girl for his son!

"You are marrying Princess Luciana," King Peter ordered. "And that is *final*."

Chapter 4

Tika admired her reflection in the water of the fountain. The baby elephant was wearing a beaded necklace and tiara and had never looked so elegant.

"The little princesses dressed me up for the Royal Engagement Ball," Tika said proudly.

"What's a ball?" Sagi wondered out loud.

Azul rolled his eyes. "Everybody knows a royal ball is big and round," Azul said. "Like a coconut."

Tika's big ears flapped back and forth as

she shook her head. "It's a big dance to congratulate Prince Antonio and Princess Luciana," she said.

Ro had no desire to go to the ball. She had been embarrassed enough in this kingdom. Besides, everyone thought she was just a strange island girl.

"That is why you need to show them you're every bit as royal as they are," Sagi said wisely.

Azul promised to teach Ro everything she needed to know about acting royal if she agreed to go to the ball. Tallulah promised to help Ro look amazing. So did Sagi.

Soon Ro found herself in Tallulah's room getting a royal fashion and beauty treatment.

"You need skirts that billow," Tallulah

said. She picked up a comb and began teasing Ro's hair. "And hair three feet high!"

Ro became dizzy as she gazed up at her towering hairdo. She tried to stand but her heavy locks made her tip forward! This look would not do.

Next was Sagi's turn. Using fresh fruit, he whipped up a hat that looked good enough to eat — but it wasn't right to wear.

Tallulah shook her head as she pulled a swath of orange material from the closet. "I know! Taffeta is the best thing," she said.

"The best thing to ignore!" Sagi scoffed.

Tallulah and Sagi fell into a tug-of-war with a piece of orange taffeta.

"Stop!" Ro told them. "There is something good in what you're saying, but I look best in island blue."

Tika's eyes darted around the room for something blue. She spotted some pretty teal curtains and pulled them off their rod.

Sagi dipped his tail into a pot of ink. With the skill of an artist, he drew a curly design on the silky material.

Tika added her own touch. Using her trunk, she picked up sparkles from a bowl of pink potpourri and blew them over the dress.

Even Azul had something to add. He used his colorful tail feathers to make a most elegant cape.

When the dress was finished, Ro gazed at her reflection in Tallulah's mirror. Not only did she look good, she felt good.

"I'm going to have a great time at the ball," Ro declared.

Meanwhile, Prince Antonio's Royal Engagement Ball had already begun. Music filled the ballroom while couples twirled across the dance floor.

Antonio and Luciana shared an awkward dance. But their conversation was even more awkward than their movements.

"I love opera," Luciana said. "Do you?"

"Not exactly," Antonio admitted. "Do you like to hike?"

"Not exactly," Luciana sighed.

Antonio excused himself politely. Then he joined his little sisters on the dance floor.

"Hold on!" Antonio chuckled. He joined hands with Gina, Rita, and Sofia and the four of them twirled in a circle. Faster and faster they went until the princesses' tiny feet were off the ground!

As he twirled, Antonio could hear a flurry of excited whispers all around him. He stopped twirling in time to see Ro sweeping down the staircase in her breathtaking teal gown.

"Is that Ro?" Rita asked.

"In the prettiest dress I've ever seen!" Sofia sighed.

Antonio was truly lovestruck. He walked across the ballroom straight to Ro.

"May I have this dance?" Antonio asked.

Ro shook her head. She was sure she could never dance like the others in the ballroom.

Antonio reminded Ro of the crocodiles she had faced down. Surely she would be able to handle a dance with him!

"I promise I won't bite," Antonio teased.

Smiling, Ro took Antonio's hands. Her feet stumbled at first, but soon she and the prince were whirling gracefully across the floor.

Queen Ariana's eyes burned as she watched the dancing couple. How dare the prince fall in love with a common island girl! She would have to speak to King Peter right away.

Outside, Ro's family of friends stood on the bridge. They could see Antonio and Ro perfectly through the castle windows.

"Ro sure looks happy," Tika sighed. But deep inside, the baby elephant was very sad. What if Ro loved Antonio more than their friendship?

Ro *was* falling in love with Antonio. And Antonio was falling deeper in love with Ro.

"Stay with me, Ro," Antonio said as the two danced in time with the music.

Ro could see Luciana on the other side of the ballroom. How could she hurt such a sweet and kind girl by stealing the person she was meant to marry?

"You and Princess Luciana belong together," Ro said. Sadly, she turned away from Antonio and hurried out of the castle.

"Why does everything have to be so complicated?" Ro said with a sigh when she found her friends.

Sagi smiled at Ro. "Life is full of change," he said. "Most of it is good, but not always easy."

Ro knew she couldn't have Prince Antonio. But she could still find out where she came from. If only she could remember her life from before she came to the island!

"I found something tonight," Sagi said.

"What?" Ro asked.

Sagi pointed to a coach parked outside the castle. On its flag was the emblem of a beautiful white rose.

"Azul and I found the same rose on a cloth that washed ashore when you came from the sea," Sagi explained. "I never thought it mattered until tonight."

Ro stared at the rose on the flag. Was it from the ship she sailed on as a child?

There was only one way to find out!

Chapter 5

With Sagi close behind, Ro raced to the coach. The coach was empty, but hitched to it was a horse waiting patiently.

"Excuse me," Ro asked the horse. "Where is this flag from?"

"The proud kingdom of Paladia," the horse replied. He went on to explain how he had brought the Duke and Duchess of Paladia to the ball that night.

Ro shivered with excitement. Could the Duke and Duchess be her parents?

"Did they have a daughter once long ago?" Ro asked, her heart pounding.

The horse replied with a shake of his mane, "No. Just three sons."

Ro's shoulders dropped. The horse's news was disappointing, but she refused to give up. Her parents had to be somewhere. All she needed was time and patience.

Meanwhile, Prince Antonio had gone to the throne room to speak with his father. He was about to get some news of his own.

"You asked to see me, Father?" Antonio asked.

"There's been a change in your wedding plans," King Peter said from his throne. "You're marrying Princess Luciana in two days."

"Two days?" Antonio cried. He had a

feeling Queen Ariana had something to do with moving up the wedding!

"I can't marry someone I don't love," Antonio said.

King Peter was not pleased. With a stern voice, he reminded Antonio of his responsibility to marry a princess. Antonio didn't want to go against his father, but how could he go against his own heart?

Antonio looked the king in the eye. "You once told me great kings make hard decisions."

"Exactly," said the king.

"This is the hardest thing I've ever done. But I can't spend the rest of my life with someone I don't love. My sisters will rule the kingdom."

The king looked angry. "Don't try my patience," he said.

"Sorry, Father," Antonio said. "I don't know any other way."

Antonio left the castle to find Ro. He stepped into the greenhouse and called out her name.

"Ro? Are you in here?"

From outside, Tika heard Antonio's voice. The baby elephant poked her head through the greenhouse door. *Now* what did the prince want?

Tika sucked in her breath as she squeezed behind a potted palm. It was a tight fit, but the perfect spot for an elephant to spy on a prince!

Antonio called Ro's name one last time. When she didn't answer, he began scribbling a note. Tika watched as Antonio stuck the note on a branch and left the greenhouse.

Tika squeezed out from behind the plant and grabbed the note with her trunk. She read it softly to herself:

"Please meet me in the rose garden tonight. Let's sail away together. Forever yours, Antonio."

Tika narrowed her eyes. So this was the prince's secret plan. Well, she could have a secret, too!

"No one is sailing away with my Ro!" Tika said. She then took Antonio's note and hid it under a big flowerpot!

Chapter 6

Tika wasn't the only one who was angry at Antonio. When Queen Ariana discovered that the prince wanted to marry Ro, she flew into a rage. But she was determined to have her daughter marry the prince. She had another plan up her sleeve, and it was a very evil one.

"I didn't think I would need to use this so soon," Queen Ariana said. She opened the lid of her trunk and smiled slyly. "But I didn't know Luciana would have a rival."

Queen Ariana pulled a small satin pouch

from the trunk. Inside the pouch was a sparkling blue powder. It was a sleeping powder!

Her plan was sinister but simple. She would feed the powder to every animal in the kingdom. After they fell into a deep, dark sleep, she would blame everything on Ro.

Queen Ariana then took out a silver cage that held three rats. They were Nat, Pat, and Matt, Ariana's faithful and sneaky servants!

"Sprinkle this powder in the food of every animal in the kingdom," Queen Ariana ordered. She then slipped the pouch over Nat's neck and ordered them to go.

Nat, Pat, and Matt scampered out of the room in search of their first victim: Queen Danielle's pet monkey, Tallulah!

They snuck into Tallulah's room and sprinkled a little of the sleeping powder into her cup. The shimmering powder swirled as it dissolved and disappeared into the warm milk.

Suddenly, the door creaked open. Nat, Pat, and Matt scurried to hide behind the thick velvet curtain. They peeked out to see Queen Danielle enter the room, carrying Tallulah.

With the help of Queen Danielle, Tallulah daintily sipped her milk. She gave a few yawns, closed her eyes, and fell into a deep sleep.

The rats slipped out of the castle unnoticed and headed for the barn. Their next victims would be the horses, sheep, and pigs. Tiny the barn swallow watched from the rafters as the rats poisoned the feed buckets. It wasn't long before every animal in the whole kingdom was fast asleep!

As the moon made way for the morning sun, the three hardworking rats trudged back to the castle. They passed the rose garden, where a brokenhearted Antonio waited alone. He had waited all night for Ro, but she never came.

Antonio dropped the rose he was saving for Ro on the dew-soaked ground. As he left the garden, he had no idea how much Ro truly cared for him. Or that a jealous little elephant by the name of Tika had hidden his note!

Chapter 7

Frantic with worry, Queen Danielle burst into the throne room.

"Peter!" Queen Danielle cried. "I can't wake up Tallulah!"

The little white monkey was limp in the queen's arms, her eyes tightly shut.

All over the kingdom, villagers were waking up to find their pets and farm animals fast asleep. Even Ro, Tika, Azul, and Sagi were surprised to find a sty full of snoozing pigs.

"Are they sick?" Ro asked.

The swallow from the barn fluttered her wings and alighted on Ro's finger. "Sick to their stomachs," she said. "I saw three rats put something in their food."

Ro followed Tiny to a bucket of slop. Taking a whiff, she recognized the smell at once.

"Sunset herb!" Ro said. Everyone on her island knew how dangerous sunset herb could be.

"Can you help the animals?" Tiny asked.

"Back home, if somebody ate sunset herb by mistake we made a rose tonic to wake them up," Ro said.

"But we don't have island roses here," Tika said.

Ro remembered the island roses in the

greenhouse. Surely Prince Antonio would let her use them for a cure!

Tika's huge ears sagged at the thought of Antonio. Maybe she should tell Ro about the hidden note.

"Ro," Tika said slowly. "About Prince Antonio . . ."

"Yes?" Ro asked.

Tika froze as all eyes turned to her. "Um . . . nothing," she said.

There was no time to lose. Ro and her animal friends hurried out of the barn to the castle. But when they tried to see Antonio, the royal butler blocked the door.

"Sorry, miss," he said. "The king insists that no one is to disturb the prince."

"Please tell him I can help," Ro said. "I can make a medicine for the animals."

"And I can dance the jig," the butler snidely replied.

Ro's heart sank as the butler shut the door. How could she help the animals when no one would let her?

Inside the castle, Queen Ariana was putting the final touches on her plot against Ro. She ran from her room and caught up with Frazer, who was hurrying down the hallway.

"On your way to see the king?" Queen Ariana asked.

Frazer nodded. "The animals are still fast asleep with no sign of waking," he said.

"I wonder how the poor animals got sick," Queen Ariana said, trying hard to seem worried.

Frazer suggested that the sickness was caused by something new in the animals' habitat. Queen Ariana reminded Frazer that there was something new — animals from the South Seas named Sagi, Azul, and Tika!

Frazer thought about this for a moment and his eyes got wide.

"Yes!" Frazer agreed. "I must tell the king!"

Queen Ariana smiled smugly as the scientist raced down the hallway. Her little plan was working like a charm.

A bad-luck charm for Ro!

When Frazer burst into the throne room, he saw many people gathered there. They had come to speak to the king about their sleeping animals.

Frazer bowed before the king and queen and said, "I'm afraid Ro may have brought the disease with her. Her animals seem

to have infected ours with a sleeping
sickness."

King Peter was concerned. But no one
was as worried as Queen Danielle.

"How do we cure Tallulah?" the queen
asked. "If she and the other animals don't
wake up soon, they'll starve!"

Frazer promised to work on a cure. In
the meantime, King Peter ordered Sagi,

Azul, and Tika to be locked up before they could do more harm.

"Guards!" King Peter called.

It wasn't long before royal guards were rounding up Ro and her animal friends and throwing them into a dark, damp dungeon!

Chapter 8

Azul's eyes darted from one stone wall to the next. "Look how low I've sunk. A royal bird languishing in this stink-hole where they keep prisoners and ruffians!"

"Are we really prisoners?" Tika asked.

A guard slipped a tray of food under the iron gate. "Food for the prisoners," he barked.

"I rest my case," Azul said with a sigh.

Ro rushed to the gate. She begged the

guard to let her speak to Prince Antonio. If the animals didn't wake up soon, they would die.

"You should have thought of that before your animals got them sick," the guard said as he walked away.

Ro didn't understand. Her friends had never made anyone sick.

"Now I know why people break out of prison," Azul said as he munched on his dinner. "The food is terrible!"

Ro and Sagi traded worried looks. What if the prison food was sprinkled with sunset herb?

"You're not eating that," Ro said slowly.

Azul opened his mouth to answer but immediately keeled over.

Ro ran to Azul. She tried to wake him up

but it was no use. The peacock was already clucking quietly in his sleep.

Ro gazed through the prison bars. She couldn't save any of the sleeping animals now. Not even one of her best friends.

When the news about Ro reached Antonio, he marched straight into the throne room to speak to his father.

"Is it true?" Antonio asked. "You threw Ro in the dungeon?"

"I had no choice," King Peter said. "Her animals are spreading disease."

Antonio didn't believe it. But there was no point in arguing with his father. He had to do something to save Ro, even if it meant sending her far, far away.

"Let Ro return to her island," Antonio said.

King Peter furrowed his eyebrows thoughtfully. "I will free Ro on one condition," he finally said. "You marry Princess Luciana."

Antonio frowned. He remembered that great kings made hard decisions. And he decided to save Ro and her friends.

"As you wish," Antonio said quietly.

The news of Antonio and Luciana's future marriage traveled quickly through the castle. When it reached Queen Ariana, she celebrated by pulling out her daughter's wedding dress.

"Your wedding dress will be the talk of the kingdom!" Queen Ariana said, fluffing out the frilly white veil.

Luciana sighed as she stroked her cat, Pearl. "The prince is in love with Ro, Mother," she said. "Not me."

Queen Ariana turned angrily to her daughter. No one was going to stop this wedding now — not even the bride!

"Enough!" Queen Ariana said angrily. "This marriage will happen. End of discussion."

"But you must want me to be happy, Mother!" Luciana protested.

Queen Ariana's lips curled in a smile as she pictured *herself* ruling the kingdom. "Oh, you will be," she cooed. "Doesn't Mama always know best?"

Luciana groaned under her breath. She knew that arguing with her mother was like arguing with the castle wall. There was no point in trying.

"Yes, Mother," Luciana sighed. Still holding Pearl, she stood up and left the room for her fitting.

"Luciana *will* marry the prince," Queen Ariana muttered to herself. With a flourish, she whipped a dark cape over her shoulders. "Whatever it takes!"

Chapter 9

The moon shone its light on the royal ship as it sailed away from Appolonia. But down in the hold where Ro and her friends sat, it was as dark as the dungeon they had just come from. The only way out of the hold was through an iron grate far above them.

While Azul slept, Ro stared up at the grate. The only way she could help Azul was if they escaped. But how could they do that? The grate was so high.

"Who would do this to Azul and all the other animals?" Tika asked.

"Somebody who wants me out of the prince's life for good," Ro decided. She knew it wasn't Princess Luciana. She was much too kind to hurt anybody. But then Ro thought of her nasty, scheming mother, Queen Ariana!

Ro knew the only hope for the animals was the island rose in the greenhouse. She studied the iron grate that kept them inside. If she could just reach it, maybe she could slide it open.

Looking around, Ro spotted a pile of wooden crates against the wall. One by one, she and Sagi slid the crates beneath the grate. Using her trunk, Tika piled the crates to make a ladder.

"Perfect," Ro said when they had finished.

Holding Azul in her arms, Ro climbed

the pile of crates. When she reached the top, she gently placed Azul down. Then carefully and quietly, she slid the grate open.

Ro held her breath as she peeked out. Two sleeping sailors snored loudly on deck. She knew they would have to slip past them in order to reach the longboat that could take them to shore.

Climbing out of the hold, Ro helped free Sagi and Tika. The ship bounced on the choppy waves as Ro led her friends to the longboat that hung from the side of the large ship.

"Help me untie it," Ro whispered.

The friends worked to untie the knots. But they didn't notice that one of the sailors was climbing the mast. A nasty gleam twinkled in the sailor's eye as he pulled out a knife. In an instant he had slashed the rigging and a boom swung loose, knocking Ro and Azul overboard!

"Ro! Azul!" Tika cried.

Waves crashed over Ro and Azul. Ro struggled to stay afloat and to keep Azul's head above the water as well. Sagi had to save his friends! He jumped into the longboat and was about to lower it into the water when the sailor pushed him overboard, too.

Horrified, Tika watched her friends as they were tossed by the waves. Before the sailor could push her in, she jumped overboard with a giant splash.

The ship sailed away into the dark night. Waves crashed all around them as Ro and her friends tried desperately to keep their heads above the icy black water.

"It's cold!" Tika cried.

"Hold on, Tika!" Sagi shouted. "Hold on!"

Hold on! The words echoed through Ro's head. Where had she heard them before? Suddenly, she remembered her father's voice calling to her as a ship sank in the distance. She was remembering herself as a child, thrashing in the waves and shouting, "Papa! Papa!"

Don't give up! her father's last words rang out in her mind. *Never give up, Rosella!*

"Rosella?" Ro whispered to herself.

Could that be her real name?

The flashbacks swept over Ro as quickly as the crashing waves. In her mind's eye, she saw herself riding the back of a dolphin — the dolphin who carried her to the island many years ago.

Ro's thoughts were interrupted by Sagi.

"Kick, Tika! Kick!" Sagi cried. "Don't give up!"

"I can't anymore!" Tika cried from the water.

Ro gasped as the baby elephant sank below the waves. "Tika, no!" she yelled. But there was no reply. As she looked frantically for Tika, Azul slipped out of her hands and began to sink below the surface as well. "Azul!" Ro called, but it no use.

Suddenly, Ro shouted, "Dolphins! If you can hear me, please help us!"

Ro waited and Sagi managed to swim to her, but all she could see were miles and miles of black water. Just as she was about

to give up, Tika rose from the water, with Azul asleep on his back and swimming dolphins under his legs.

Ro took hold of Sagi and held him close as one more dolphin lifted her out of the water. Ro clutched her friend as she rode the swimming dolphin's back.

"Thank you!" Ro said.

The dolphin chattered a chipper, "No problem!"

Ro and her friends rode the dolphins all the way to shore. The kind animals had saved their lives. Now it was up to Ro to save the other animals!

Chapter 10

Ro stood on the shore and waved good-bye to the dolphins.

"Is it true, Ro?" Tika asked. "You really remember everything from before?"

"Not everything," Ro admitted. "But maybe enough to find my family."

Tika begged Ro not to go to the greenhouse for the rose tonic. What if they were caught and thrown back in the dungeon? But Ro insisted on saving Azul and the other sleeping animals.

"You may not be a princess to the king

and queen," Sagi said proudly, "but you're a princess in my eyes."

Sagi's words pierced Tika's heart. Sniffing back tears, Tika confessed to hiding the prince's note from Ro in the greenhouse.

"Why didn't you tell me?" Ro asked.

"I didn't want you to leave me," Tika cried. "If you marry the prince, you won't love your friends as much."

Ro smiled as she gave the baby elephant a great big hug.

"Tika, when you joined our family, do you think I loved Sagi and Azul less?"

"I don't know," answered the little elephant.

"I didn't love them less. I still loved them with all my heart. If we make room for someone else, it doesn't mean there's less for you," Ro explained. "It only means our circle has grown."

Tika gave it some thought. Then her frown turned into a smile.

"You'll always be my Tika," Ro said.

"And you'll always be my Ro!" Tika said happily.

Ro and her family of friends began to make their way to the greenhouse. They had no idea that a certain wicked queen had already gotten there.

Queen Ariana was looking around the enormous greenhouse. She gazed at the tables set for the wedding reception — and the grandest wedding cake she had ever seen! But she did not notice Tiny watching her from inside a flowerpot.

Nat, Pat, and Matt popped out from under the tablecloth. They watched as their mistress reached under her cape for the sleeping powder.

"From me to you, Antonio," Queen Ariana snickered. "You and your parents will sleep for a very, very long time."

As Queen Ariana sprinkled sleeping powder all over the cake, she remembered a time long ago when she was just a child. At that time her family had tried to harm the king. But they were caught and as punishment the family was banished from the kingdom and forced to live on a pig farm. Ariana grew up hating pigs. She also grew up wanting *revenge*.

When she was older, Ariana found a king of her own and married him. Together, they had a child, and Ariana came up with a plan: She would marry her daughter off to Prince Antonio. Then she would destroy the royal family that had punished *her* family!

It was a very wicked plan. But Ariana was a very wicked queen!

Queen Ariana sprinkled the last of the powder and it disappeared into the frosting, leaving no trace of its presence.

"And while they sleep, Luciana, the new queen, shall rule the kingdom," Queen Ariana declared. "And who rules Luciana?"

Three ratty paws pointed to Ariana.

"Her Royal Magnificence!" Nat said. "That's who!"

Queen Ariana laughed wickedly as she hid the pouch beneath her cape. She had a wedding to attend. And an entire royal family to destroy!

"Now," Queen Ariana said, "I must

remember to tell Luciana not to eat any cake."

Tiny ducked beneath the flowers as Queen Ariana left the greenhouse. She had seen Queen Ariana's blue powder before. It was the same powder the rats sprinkled in the barn animals' feed!

While Queen Ariana and the guests filed into the ballroom for the wedding ceremony, Ro slipped into the greenhouse.

When she saw the wedding cake, Ro frowned. But she knew she had no time to be sad. She had to concoct the rose tonic and save the sleeping animals.

"We'd better get started," Ro said. "We have to make the tonic. I need the petals of an island rose, coconut milk, and the leaves of a white star vine."

Just then, Tiny the barn swallow flitted onto Ro's shoulder. She began chirping softly into her ear. Ro's eyes grew wide with alarm as Tiny told her of Queen Ariana's horrible plan. She knew she needed to work quickly.

Tika and Sagi helped to fetch the ingredients, and Ro got right to work.

Suddenly, the castle guards stormed into the greenhouse and spotted Ro holding a bowl before the sleeping peacock.

"You're under arrest!" shouted a guard.

Ro froze with the bowl in her hands. If she was going to help the animals, she would have to think fast!

Chapter 11

Ro kept her eyes on the guards as she passed the bowl of tonic to Sagi. "Find Tallulah and see if this works," she whispered.

Sagi balanced the bowl between his paws. He slipped out of the greenhouse, but he did not get very far.

"Get the beast!" a guard ordered.

It was now up to Tika to get help. She barreled between the guards and charged out of the greenhouse toward the castle, trumpeting all the way!

Inside the grand ballroom, the wedding

of Prince Antonio and Princess Luciana was already under way. The couple gazed sadly at the minister as he spoke in a booming voice.

"We are gathered here to join in matrimony Princess Luciana to His Highness, Prince Antonio."

At last! Queen Ariana thought, grinning slyly.

"If someone objects to this union," the minister spoke on, "speak now."

The doors burst open and Tika charged in. Shocked whispers filled the room as the trumpeting baby elephant ran down the aisle.

"What's happening?"

"Is that an elephant?"

"What's it doing here?"

Rita, Sofia, and Gina were happy to see Tika. But Antonio was puzzled.

"What is it, Tika?" Antonio asked.

Tika tugged at Antonio's arm with her trunk. The others followed as the baby elephant led Antonio out of the ballroom to the greenhouse. The guards were just leading Ro to the dungeon when Antonio and the others charged in.

"Release her at once!" Antonio ordered.

The guards obeyed the prince and dropped Ro's arms. Antonio turned to see his parents standing in the doorway.

"What do you think you're doing, Antonio?" King Peter demanded.

"We had a deal, Father," Antonio said. "I'd marry Princess Luciana and Ro would go free."

Queen Ariana pushed her way through the crowd. She pointed her finger at Ro and said, "This wild girl and her animals are spreading disease!"

"No we aren't," Ro insisted. "Somebody put an herb in the animals' food and I can cure them with a healing tonic."

"Why should we trust you?" King Peter asked.

That very moment Sagi burst in with Tallulah. The little white monkey was wide awake and totally recovered!

"Thank you, Ro!" Tallulah said with a smile.

A joyous Queen Danielle hugged her beloved pet. "Maybe it's true," she said. "Maybe Ro does have a cure."

"But if Ro didn't cause the sickness,"

King Peter said, "who put the herb in the animals' food?"

"Queen Ariana," Ro blurted.

The guests gasped with surprise. How dare a common girl accuse a queen?

"She put the sunset herb in the wedding cake, too," Ro said.

"Now everyone can see how crazy you

are." Queen Ariana laughed. "Who told you this — a little birdie?"

The guests laughed out loud, too, but Ro remained calm.

"If I'm so crazy, you won't mind eating some cake," Ro said.

Queen Ariana scowled as Antonio moved to the cake, cut a big piece, and held it out to her with a fork.

"Please, have a bite," said Antonio.

The queen took a forkful of cake but paused before putting it in her mouth. "You probably put something in the cake yourself to frame me," Queen Ariana snapped.

Luciana stepped forward. "She didn't, Mother," she said.

Queen Ariana looked sternly at Luciana. "Luciana, think," she snapped.

Luciana looked at her mother for a moment and then continued. "Before the wedding you told me not to eat any cake. Remember?"

The wicked queen knew she was foiled and decided to make a run for it. She shoved the cake table at Ro and Antonio. Then she barreled her way through the crowd and out of the greenhouse.

"She won't get far," Antonio declared. "After her!"

Chapter 12

Queen Ariana jumped onto a guest's carriage and snapped the reins hard. The team of horses reared back. Their hooves thundered on the ground as they shot off.

Antonio raced down the path after Queen Ariana. Before she could get far, he managed to jump on the back of the stolen carriage.

Queen Ariana glared back at Antonio. Snapping the reins harder, she rode the carriage over the bridge just as a lovely young guest was crossing over. The girl jumped aside to avoid the carriage but as she did, she slipped and fell over the side of the bridge.

Antonio wanted to pursue Queen Ariana, but he couldn't ignore the guest — she needed his help. When he saw the young woman fall off the bridge, he leaped off the carriage and hoped he would not be too late. Looking over the side of the bridge, Antonio spotted the guest dangling dangerously by her fingertips from the trestle.

"Take my hand!" Antonio called to her.

The frightened girl took Antonio's hand and he pulled her safely onto the bridge. He was relieved that she was safe but his heart sank when he looked up just in time to see Queen Ariana ride away.

Antonio was disappointed, but just then Ro appeared. She was riding on Tika's back and the two of them were gaining quickly on Queen Ariana.

As the elephant approached the carriage, Ro reached up and broke off a tree branch. Steadily, she aimed the branch at one of the spinning carriage wheels. When the time was right, Ro hurled the stick. Like a javelin, it whizzed through the air and hit its mark perfectly!

The carriage tipped as the wheel jammed. Queen Ariana screamed as she tumbled off the carriage into a sloppy pigsty!

Groaning under her breath, Queen Ariana sat up. She was covered in mud. Her worst nightmare had come true. She was surrounded by snoring, dirty pigs again!

"Get away from me!" Queen Ariana yelled as the pigs rolled in her direction. "Get away from me!"

Ro smiled. She was glad they had stopped Queen Ariana in her tracks. But the sleeping pigs reminded her that she had work to do.

Everyone returned to the greenhouse to watch Ro concoct more of the rose tonic. As she mixed the ingredients, Ro could see Antonio and Luciana trading smiles.

"They make a beautiful couple," Ro sighed.

"Then why is the prince coming over here?" Tika asked.

Ro looked up. Antonio *was* walking over. He stopped before Ro and gazed into her eyes.

"Sail away with me, Ro," Antonio said.

"I can't do that," Ro said. "Princess Luciana —"

"— wants us to be happy," Antonio cut in. The prince suddenly got down on one knee. He took a deep breath and spoke the words he had waited to say for a long, long time. "Ro, will you marry me?"

Chapter 13

Ro stared at Antonio, too excited to speak.

"Say yes," Tika said, nudging Ro.

When Ro finally found her voice, she blurted out, "Yes. Yes, yes, yes!"

Antonio swept Ro into his arms.

Just then, King Peter appeared. "Excuse me," he said, interrupting Antonio and Ro's celebration.

"Father," Antonio said seriously, "no more nonsense about me marrying a princess."

The king looked at Antonio and Ro for

a moment before speaking. He sighed. "Perhaps it is time for a change. Welcome, Ro," King Peter said with a smile.

"Please, call me Rosella," Ro said. "That's my real name."

"Rosella?" a voice spoke.

Everyone turned as one of the royal guests stepped out of the crowd. When Ro saw her, she couldn't help feeling that she knew this woman. But from where? Or when?

"Your name is Rosella?" the woman asked.

"Yes," Ro said. She could feel her heart pounding inside her chest.

"I am Marissa, queen of Paladia," the woman said.

The queen's words filled Ro's heart with joy. She began singing the lullaby she remembered from so many years ago. . . .

"'Sun goes down and we're here together. Stay with me and you can dream forever.'"

Happy tears filled Queen Marissa's eyes as she joined in singing, "'It's magic when you are here beside me . . . close your eyes and let me hold you tight.'"

Rosella and Queen Marissa sang the lullaby together word for word. When it was over, they fell into each other's arms.

Sagi and Tika looked at each other and smiled. Ro had found her mother at last. And if her mother was a queen, that made Ro something she was always meant to be: a princess!

💗　💗　💗

In just a few weeks, the kingdom of Appolonia had a new wedding to celebrate. Luscious flowers decorated the gazebo as Gina, Rita, and Sofia scattered rose petals on the long red carpet that led to the altar. Ro looked stunning in her white wedding dress as she rode Tika down the aisle.

"You'll always be my Tika," Ro whispered.

"And you'll always be my Ro," Tika whispered back.

Before the eyes of the kingdom, Antonio and Rosella exchanged rings and promises.

Later, as the royal ship set sail to take Ro and Antonio on a wonderful honeymoon, Ro knew she had a wonderful new life awaiting her. A life fit for a prince and an island princess.

And they would surely live happily ever after!

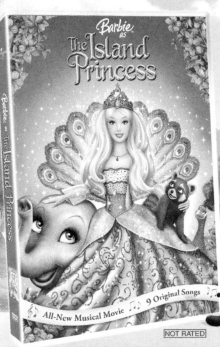